Ziggy McFinster's
Nantucket Adventure

by C. R. Bagley

Illustrations by Nadine Bernard Westcott

VOLT PRESS

11 10 09 08 07   5 4 3 2 1

Library of Congress Cataloging-in-Publication Data

Bagley, Conor.
Ziggy McFinster's Nantucket Adventure / by Conor Bagley; illustrations by Nadine Bernard Westcott.
p. cm.
Summary: Ziggy McFinster, a snake that can magically transform himself into any animal, takes his wife, Bitsy,
to the island of Nantucket on a honeymoon filled with adventure.
ISBN 978-1-56625-315-4
1. Nantucket Island (Mass.)--Juvenile fiction. [1. Nantucket Island (Mass.)--Fiction. 2. Snakes--Fiction. 3. Magic--Fiction. 4. Adventure and
adventurers--Fiction. 5. Honeymoons--Fiction.] I. Westcott, Nadine Bernard, ill. II. Title.

PZ7.B14029Zig 2007
[E]--dc22

2007021998

VOLT PRESS
a division of Bonus Books, Inc.
9255 W. Sunset Blvd., #711
Los Angeles, CA 90069
www.volt-press.com

Bonus Books/Volt Press titles may also be purchased at special **quantity discounts** for educational, business or promotional use.
For more information please contact our Special Orders Department at **(877) 660-1960** or **specialorders@bonusbooks.com**.

Book Design by E. Friedman

Printed in the U.S.A.

To my Mom and Dad and my sister, Vaughan,
who all love Nantucket as much as I do.

And to our dog, Riley,
who first inspired me to love animals.

CHAPTER 1
OFF TO NANTUCKET!

I, Ziggy McFinster, am a magical snake. A magical snake who loves a good adventure!

I have always been especially curious about the beautiful island of Nantucket, off the coast of Massachusetts. So my lovely wife Bitsy and I decided that we would like to have our honeymoon there. This was going to be my one getaway from my "duty to Mother Nature." Since I have remarkable powers to shape-shift into any animal, I have to use my abilities to save plants and animals around the world.

"Ziggy," said my wife. "We have to start swimming to Nantucket now." I love my beautiful Bitsy lots, although she can be a bit bossy at times. I met her in New York City along with Gordo, who is my best friend. He is an elf from the North Pole, who needs to cut back on the fries a bit. He married a pretty South Pole elf, named Zegalega. They live near to us in Delaware, but they are taking their honeymoon in Bermuda while we're in Nantucket.

"Ziggy . . . Ziggy McFINSTER!

"I'm coming, honey!" I replied and we set off for the beach.

Whenever I want to change into an animal, I have to *think* just like that animal! So in order to get into the mind-set of a dolphin, I thought about fish and all the great wonders of the sea. I thought about what it would be like to swim and play in the waves. I felt myself getting bigger, and a dorsal fin started to grow from the middle of my back! As all my rough scales fell off, my skin became rubbery and smooth, like a rubber ball. Bitsy slithered onto my back and wrapped herself around my fin for dear life, as we set out on our voyage to Nantucket.

At first, I forgot Bitsy was on my back, and I dove into the water. But after a bit, I learned to jump on the surface of the water. I was very warm under my dolphin skin, though Bitsy must have been cold from the wind and water! The journey seemed to go on forever, but it really only took a few days. Once we saw the Sankaty Lighthouse, we knew we had reached our destination.

CHAPTER 2

THE gigantic flying object

When we reached the lighthouse, Bitsy decided that she didn't want to stay on the 'Sconset bluff because of her fear of heights. So we swam along the coast, and finally found land that was nearer to sea level.

I transformed back to my old, scaly self. As we were moving up the beach, we saw a seagull caught in a fishing net, and we immediately rushed to his assistance. Deeply grateful, he said his name was Sworgy the Seagull. We talked for a while, but since we were very tired, I told him that we'd see him soon.

We stayed hidden in the dunes for the night. When we woke up, we had the most intense hunger imaginable and headed towards town. As we got near town, Bitsy noticed something in the sky and said, "Look, Ziggy! Look at that big bird coming toward us!"

"Sweetie," I said, "I don't think that's a bird…"

We soon realized . . . we were on the Nantucket Airport runway!

The gigantic flying object soared downward, landed on the runway . . . and headed toward us! *Quickly*, I might add - my life flashed before my eyes! I realized that the plane was too wide for us to dodge, but too high for me to fly over it. I knew that the only way for us to avoid the plane was to go under it.

Bitsy and I lay flat against the pavement as the massive machine roared toward us. I heard a big "WHOOSH!" as the wheels *just missed us!* Even though we were safe from harm, that was just about the scariest thing that had ever happened to us.

I couldn't imagine what would have happened if we hadn't managed to dodge it. Where would we be? We were pretty shaken up by the terror of that monstrosity, and it took us a while to get that close call out of our minds.

After our unexpected airport adventure, we were ready to start our honeymoon on Nantucket. We were still quite hungry, and had a big craving for baked goods, so we rushed into town to find a bakery.

NANTUCKET BAKE SHOP

CHAPTER 3
AROUND TOWN

In order to be safe from the humans in town, I turned into one myself. My transformation wasn't that different from turning into a monkey. Except that my feet were more like feet instead of hands, and I only seemed to have hair in certain places! I then put Bitsy in a little picnic basket, which had holes to allow her to see and breathe.

We jumped into a cab and told the driver that we had to get to a bakery as fast as possible! He dropped us off at the Nantucket Bake Shop on Orange Street. When I opened the screen door, the sweet aroma of freshly baked dough filled my nose. Although it seemed like a huge bakery at first, it was actually just one little room. On our right, we saw many different types of colorful cakes-and on our left, we found cookies of all shapes and sizes. Just looking at all the goodies made my mouth water. There were glazed mouse ears, cinnamon diamonds sprinkled with sugar, and those "Magees" were chocolate heaven!

Once we had tasted a little bit of everything, we remembered the cab driver telling us Main Street was the major street on Nantucket. We followed Orange Street until we reached Main. We first wanted to go hear some music, but once we came upon Mitchell's Book Corner, we knew we wanted to stop and look around the store!

Most of the books we saw there were about Nantucket, such as *Nat, Nat, the Nantucket Cat* and many others. Some of them were novels that everyone had read, such as *Harry Potter*. Bitsy didn't know how to speak English, much less read, and as a human, I could only read light children's books. This problem forced us to buy only kids' books, and since we still needed a map of Nantucket, we picked up one of those, too.

When Bitsy and I were done with our shopping, she said she wanted to stay in a nice room for the night and have a fine dinner. So I took her to The White Elephant Hotel. Like most of the houses on Nantucket, the hotel was gray. I had noticed that most of the houses were made of gray shingles and many had what appeared to be chimneys. I learned that these were actually called *widows' walks.* These were originally for sailors' wives to go up and look for their husbands' ships as they arrived home from their whaling adventures.

I planned to dine with Bitsy at the lovely Brant Point Grill that looked over the harbor, but then I remembered that she was a *snake,* which probably wouldn't go over well with humans at the restaurant. So instead, I took her to our room where we ordered room service! We ate steak, potatoes, and a yummy hot-fudge sundae for dessert. With food in our bellies, we got into our gigantic hotel bed and went to sleep.

The next morning, we lazed around our hotel room, overlooking the harbor. It was nice to relax. We slithered around the room playing hide-and-seek (Bitsy ALWAYS wins!) and eating everything out of the little refrigerator. *That stuff is free, isn't it? ? ?*

 THE MYSTERIOUS STRANGER

Eventually, Bitsy and I decided to go out for a walk, so I transformed myself into a human again. As we left the hotel, I suddenly noticed a strange man standing across the street, staring at me. We started walking down Main Street and every time I turned around, the man would duck into a store to hide. What was up with this guy, I wondered? He looked a little scary, to be honest. The man was tall, skinny, and had a long moustache that needed trimming.

Carrying Bitsy in my basket, I walked into a gift shop called The Hub. I asked the lady at the cash register, "Excuse me, ma'am. Do you know who that man is, over there?" as I pointed him out across the street.

"Why, yes, that's Charlie O'Trigger. Stay away from him, though. He's bad news!"

"What does he do?" I asked.

"Oh, he likes to hang out at Pudley's Pub, watch television, and do nothing all day."

I started to become concerned, and decided it was time for another transformation. I quickly walked to Straight Wharf with Bitsy safe in her basket, turned myself into a dolphin, and dove into the ocean.

I made that last change in the nick of time. For some reason, I felt we just had to escape from this O'Trigger fellow! What did I ever do to him?

Bitsy had some trouble holding her breath while wrapped around one of my fins, but she managed. Once we were out of sight of the strange man, I flipped Bitsy up onto my dorsal fin. As we swam out of the Nantucket Harbor, I began to tell Bitsy about the disappointing dream I had had the night before . . .

CHAPTER 5

THE DEMANDING DREAM

I explained to Bitsy that a mysterious lady had spoken to me in my dream:

"ZIGGY McFINSTER!" the lady exclaimed. *"You have not been doing your duty during your stay on Nantucket. You must help Mother Nature EVERYWHERE you go! You can start by lowering the population of deer on the island. They are trampling and destroying plants. Your duty is to talk to the deer, and tell them to 'chill out!' Mother Nature will reward you."*

So, I told Bitsy that after I had this telling dream, I knew I needed to talk to all of the deer on Nantucket . . . and show them who's boss.

Bitsy was not pleased to hear this in the middle of our honeymoon.

"Ziggy McFinster! You promised me a relaxing, stress-free vacation. I'm so sick of our plans being affected by YOUR 'duty to Mother Nature!' What ever happened to the charming, *romantic* Ziggy I used to know?"

"C'mon, honey, it's only a few deer. I'll be back finishing our vacation with you in no time."

To tell you the truth, I had no idea how long all this deer business was going to take, but I was hoping it wouldn't be too long. I tried to distract Bitsy from the topic by pointing out how close we were to our destination.

"Look, Bit . . . we're almost at Eel Point!"

We glided through the water in sulky silence until we were on the sandy beaches of Eel Point. Back on shore, I shape-shifted from a dolphin back into my own, snaky self, and Bitsy apologized. She said she was sorry for being selfish, and agreed that my duty to Mother Nature was more important than our romantic getaway.

The sand felt warm against our skins. We appreciated the sun's rays beating down on us after a cold swim in the ocean. The lapping waves relaxed us into a tranquil state, and we wanted a nice long nap. Soon, reality set in, and we knew we needed to find a place to stay for the night before we collapsed on the soft, dreamy sand. We hid amongst the plants, to make sure we could not be seen.

I woke up early to find deer before sunrise. My plan was simple: I would turn into one of them and run among them in their herd. I would then encourage them to eat more and more plants and flowers, until they filled their bellies. Then, this would make them so sick that they would surely pledge to never eat another flower or plant again, except for the certain species that I would recommend to them! And since deer are active early in the morning and at night, I figured I could take care of this and still spend quality time with Bitsy during the rest of the day.

Every morning and every night I continued to follow my plan, and after just a few days, I knew I had succeeded. I had managed to talk to every deer, and they understood and agreed to chill out. Relieved, I changed back into a snake, and slithered back to Bitsy.

We could now focus on relaxing again. Bitsy was thrilled we could finish our vacation together. No more problems, no more worries . . . it was going to be a breeze!

CHAPTER 6

A Very Close Call

We wanted to see more of the island, so we decided to rent a bike. Of course, snakes can't ride bikes, so I transformed into a human again and went to Young's Bicycle Shop. Some people recommended crabbing at the Madaket creeks, so I headed there with Bitsy in my bicycle basket. But first we stopped at *Something Natural* for roast beef sandwiches and orange mango-flavored Nantucket Nectars.

We traveled on Cliff Road, which led us to the Madaket Road. The bike path curved over little hills, and I enjoyed taking my feet off the pedals and letting the wind rush through my hair as we coasted downhill. Then we passed through a forest . . . the view was incredible! When we emerged from the shade, the sunlight shone brightly on our skin. We could see the clear blue water, and the marshy grasses of the creeks.

I put our bike aside and headed down towards the pond. We had to cross a bridge, and we saw there were a few openings in the bush where we could crab. I attached some raw chicken meat to a string and put the bait in the water.

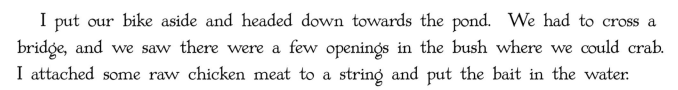

After a long while at the pond, Bitsy slithered off to find us something to eat.

Then suddenly, I heard a snake-like yelp! I ran deep into the bushes, and who should I discover, but ...Charlie O'Trigger! And he was pointing a gun at Bitsy!

"Allow me to introduce myself," he said gruffly. "I'm Charlie."

"Hello, Charlie. I'm Ziggy. Ziggy McFinster."

"You two were spotted dodging a plane on the runway at the airport," Charlie said. "It's autumn hunting season, and since they don't want a new breed of snakes around here, there is a $1,000 reward for your capture! DEAD...OR ALIVE."

"What do you mean?" I said nervously. This is my *pet* snake, Bitsy."

"Heh, heh, you can't trick ME," he said nastily. "I saw you down by Eel Point. I know you can shift into different animals! Now, turn into a snake...before I pull this trigger!"

In a risky move, I blurted out, "Make me!"

Angrily, he started to load his gun...and so I quickly did as he wished. It seemed all hope was lost. Just then, Bitsy looked up and said, "Look, Ziggy! There's another plane coming toward us!"

"Sweetie," I said, "I don't think that's a plane..."

I immediately realized…it was Sworgy the Seagull, and he was swooping down at Charlie!

BANG!
BANG!

Startled, we realized that Charlie had shot his gun! But Sworgy saved the day, as he had managed to swipe the gun from his grasp! The gun flew through the air and landed on the ground next to me. I turned into a human again, and pointed the gun at Charlie.

"Leave us alone for the rest of our trip," I yelled. "And if I ever see you again, it's not going to be a happy ending. Now, *get lost!*"

Charlie stomped out to Madaket Road and stuck his thumb up to hitch a ride. A car stopped, but before he got inside, he turned back to say:

"Mark my words. This is not the last you'll see of me. *I will hunt you down, Ziggy McFinster!*"

He slammed the door, and the car drove away. Thankfully, that was the last we saw of Charlie O'Trigger for the rest of our stay on Nantucket.

farewell (for now)

To express our gratitude, we invited the heroic Sworgy to come to Great Point with us. When I transformed into a seagull, Sworgy looked shocked! I explained my special abilities to our confused friend. Then, we told him about our wild adventures on Nantucket and we set off for Great Point.

From high in the sky, Sworgy, Bitsy and I took in a spectactular view, as we could see every part of the island. We could see Eel Point all the way to 'Sconset. We could see Madaket Beach all the way to Great Point. The houses looked so small, and the people...they looked like tiny ants! The ferry looked more like a toy boat in a bathtub than something large enough to transport hundreds of people! We flew over Coatue and noticed the little trails that the boats left behind. The salty wind was rushing through my seagull feathers.

Finally, we arrived at Great Point and landed on top of the lighthouse to scout out a place for us to spend a day at the beach. In the distance, I could see the perfect spot.

Some people out swimming had left their food unprotected, so while Bitsy sunned herself, Sworgy and I scavenged food from various picnics, as seagulls do. We pecked at plastic bags and brought bread, sandwiches, and chips back to Bitsy. I turned back into my snake self and settled in to enjoy our picnic with my bride and our new, feathered friend.

Later, after a fine day of sunning and feasting, it was time to say goodbye to Nantucket. I asked Bitsy what she thought of the idea of flying back to Delaware.

"Oh! What a thoughtful husband. How nice that this time, I won't have to endure the cold, salty water. You're such a romantic, Ziggy."

(I hadn't even thought of that, but it's always good to get credit for being a good husband.)

After thanking Sworgy once more and saying our goodbyes, I shape-shifted into an eagle and helped Bitsy to wriggle up onto my back. The two of us flew serenely into the sunset, filled with fond memories of our unexpectedly adventurous honeymoon on Nantucket!